This edition published by Kids Can Press in 2019
Originally published in French under the title *Le jardin de Jaco*

© 2018 Casterman
Text and illustrations by Marianne Dubuc

English translation © 2019 Kids Can Press

Kids Can Press gratefully acknowledges the financial support
of the Government of Ontario, through Ontario Creates;
the Ontario Arts Council; the Canada Council for the Arts;
and the Government of Canada for our publishing activity.

Published in Canada and the U.S. by Kids Can Press Ltd.
25 Dockside Drive, Toronto, ON M5A 0B5

Kids Can Press is a Corus Entertainment Inc. company

www.kidscanpress.com

The text is set in Calibri.

English edition edited by Yvette Ghione

Printed and bound in China in 12/2018 by RR Donnelley Asia Printing Solutions Limited

CM 19 0 9 8 7 6 5 4 3 2 1

Library and Archives Canada Cataloguing in Publication

Dubuc, Marianne, 1980–
[Jardin de Jaco. English]
       And then the seed grew / [written and illustrated by]
Marianne Dubuc.

Translation of: Le jardin de Jaco.

ISBN 978-1-5253-0207-7 (hardcover)

       I. Title. II. Title: Jardin de Jaco. English.

PS8607.U2245J3713 2019   jC843'.6   C2018-905925-7

Marianne Dubuc

and then the SEED grew

Kids Can Press

Once there was a garden. It was an ordinary garden filled with flowers and plants, where many creatures lived all year round.

Some lived aboveground, like Mr. Gnome and little Jack. And some lived underground, like Yvonne the mole, the Field Mouse family, Paulie the earthworm and Colette the ant. Everyone was quite content. Until …

One morning, out of the blue, something fell from the sky.
At first, no one took notice except for an unhappy Jack,
whose hat was crushed by the falling thing.

The thing was a seed.

And soon the seed began to grow.

With a *crick!* its seed coat split open, and out popped a small root.

Underground, Colette and her ant friends were annoyed: the root was blocking their path. If they were going to arrive home in time for tea, they would need to find a way around.

Yvonne noticed a small crack in her bathroom ceiling. *No cause for worry*, she thought. *A few taps of my hammer should do the trick.*

But no sooner had she fetched her toolbox than disaster struck: there was now a root poking out of a hole where the small crack had been! Yvonne quickly sprung into action to fix it.

At the same moment, Mr. Gnome noticed a new plant aboveground.

What's this growing in the garden? he wondered. He wanted to ask Colette, but she was too busy digging new tunnels around the plant's roots.

As the days passed, the plant continued to grow.

Yvonne was growing more and more upset. She was on her third round of repairs.

Things weren't much better in the Field Mouse house. No sooner had Susie made a wish and blown out her birthday candles than her party was ruined by the invading roots.

As for the ants, all of the detours they had to take to go about their work in the garden left them exhausted.

Night and day, the plant grew.

Yvonne gave up on her renovations — the bathroom was a mess, and she was worn out.

The Field Mouse house had been overrun. They had no choice but to move. All of the neighbors lent a hand — even Paulie, who usually kept to himself.

Everyone was fed up. Underground and aboveground, the plant was wreaking havoc all through the garden.

Yvonne's bathroom was permanently out of order, Mr. Gnome was trapped in his house, the ants were detour-dizzy and the poor field mice had to move yet again. Something had to be done!

The garden residents held an emergency meeting.

"My bathroom is unusable!" complained Yvonne.

"Where will we live?" Mr. Field Mouse worried.

"We can't get home!" cried the ants.

"This is unbearable!" exclaimed Mr. Gnome, who had finally managed to escape.

They all agreed that there was only one thing to do:
cut the plant down.

Everyone had a task. Yvonne, the expert tunnel-digger, would excavate the roots. The tireless ants would eat and mulch the leaves. And the sharp-toothed mice would cut the stalk.

Just as Mr. Field Mouse prepared to take the first bite, someone called out:

"WAIT!"

It was little Jack.

"Is this plant really so terrible?"
Jack asked gently.

"Hasn't its shade kept Mr. Gnome's house cool
and comfortable? And wouldn't the field mouselings
have great fun climbing its branches?

"From its highest leaves,
the ants could easily map out
their routes in the garden!

"And don't forget its fruit ..."

"Fruit?!" everyone cried in surprise.
Then, looking up, they discovered ... tomatoes!

Inspired by Jack's words, the garden residents decided to let the plant be. Soon they all learned to appreciate its many merits and were quite content once again.

Yvonne and the field mice were glad to be neighbors. Colette and the ant colony now had a vast network of tunnels and a handy lookout in the plant's highest leaves.

And Paulie? He had made a friend.

So the following spring, it was with great excitement that the garden inhabitants made another discovery: *three* new seeds!